VERY MERRY
Christmas
TALES

Other holiday titles you may enjoy:

The Santa Paws series
By Nicholas Edwards

Santa Claus, Inc.
Santa S.O.S
The Santa Solution
The Santa Contest
The Santa Season
By Linda Ford

Rover Saves Christmas
By Roddy Doyle

VERY MERRY Christmas TALES

SCHOLASTIC INC.

New York Toronto London Auckland Sydney
Mexico City New Delhi Hong Kong Buenos Aires

ISBN 0-439-68514-1

Designed by Jennifer Rinaldi Windau

12 11 10 9 8 7 6 5 4 3 2 1   4 5 6 7 8 9/0

Printed in the U.S.A.

First printing, November 2004

VERY MERRY Christmas TALES

Contents

WALLY'S FIRST CHRISTMAS

By Barbara Seuling

The boxes sat in the middle of the living room floor. They made Wally nervous. And that made him scratch.

"Mom!" shouted Lindsey. "Wally is scratching again."

"Get the flea powder!" Lindsey's mom called. "That's all we need — another flea infestation."

Flea infestation? Couldn't a dog have a natural itch now and then? Wally couldn't imagine having a single flea. Not since that flea bath he had before he left the Safe Haven Doggy Shelter. And he wouldn't have had them at all, had it not been for that cat that Lindsey found in the street. That cat's fleas had jumped ship — or cat — and leaped onto him the minute they got inside the house.

Before he knew what hit him, Wally was engulfed in a white powder cloud. *ACHOO!* He shook his body, but the powder made him sneeze again. *A-CHOO-OOO!* The spray went everywhere.

"Ee-yew!" cried Lindsey. "That was gross, Wally!" She wiped her face with her sleeve.

Well, what did you expect me to do? Stop breathing? With his ears down and his tail between his legs, Wally loped over to his bed by the fireplace and flopped down. He stared at those hateful boxes.

The last time there were boxes around, the family Wally lived with had moved, and they didn't take him with them to their new home. So Wally went to the Safe Haven Doggy Shelter. That's where Lindsey had found him. That was just a few short weeks ago.

Lindsey let him sleep on her bed and fussed over him and played with him every day. They were still getting to know each other. But now it looked like the same thing was happening all over again. Why did people have to move around so much? He would be happy just to stay put with a person of his own. Preferably in a place without a cat.

Wally stretched lazily, until his paws extended as far as they would go. Then he tried to relax. He closed his eyes, but he couldn't sleep. He had too much on his mind.

It wasn't just those boxes. The family seemed to be going crazy. That afternoon, Lindsey's dad had come into the house dragging a real live tree, the kind that Wally knew very well from the backyard. Naturally curious, he had walked over to it, given it a good sniff, and, like he would with any good tree, lifted his leg.

Well! You would have thought he had torn up the furniture, as he'd done at his very first home. Everyone yelled at once:

"NO, WALLY!"

"BAD DOG, WALLY!"

"STOP, WALLY!"

Wally hardly had time to put his leg down before they were on top of him. Alarmed, he skittered off to the bathroom — his "time-out" place.

Later, when it was all clear, he came out to find the tree standing in the living room with lights all over it. Funny little toys hung from the branches. Lindsey was up on a ladder putting a big glittery star on the very top of the tree.

Wally found a toy near his bed and sniffed it. Lindsey had given him several toys since he came to live with her. This one wasn't like the others. It was brightly colored and had a string on the end of it. Wally liked the smell, so he licked it. It didn't have much of an odor and the taste wasn't much, either, but it looked like it would be fun to chew. He grabbed it in his teeth and crunched down on it.

Wally was nibbling at his new toy contentedly when Lindsey saw him and screamed, "Oh, no, Wally!" She swept down to grab it from him.

"Aw, Mom," she said sadly. "It's the penguin ornament that you got on your last trip. Wally chewed the head off."

Lindsey's mom looked like she might cry. "I loved that penguin," she said.

What is she so upset about? It didn't even squeak. Wally thought his plastic hot dog with the squeaker was a much better toy.

But he knew better than to hang around when people were upset with him. He went to his bed and settled down. He would never figure people out.

The cat came sauntering out at that very moment. He walked close to Wally, close enough to really annoy him. The cat put a paw on the bed and looked around. Wally didn't bark. He would show them he could control himself.

"Aw," said Lindsey's mom. "Mikey is trying to make friends." Wally tensed up, watching the little furball climb onto his bed. His tail sashayed right in front of Wally's nose. Wally could have grabbed it in one move, but he didn't. He lay very still, his chin on his paws, his skin twitching, and kept his eyes on the cat as it curled up and settled down by his side.

Wally was so tense that when the cat swatted him with his tail, he jumped up in surprise. The cat went flying under the tree. Wally dashed after it.

"Watch out!" Lindsey warned. The tree came crashing down, lights, ornaments, and all. Several ornaments broke in the fall.

Everyone stared at Wally.

What are you looking at me for? It was the cat's fault, didn't you see?

Lindsey's mom yanked him by the collar and whisked him off to the bathroom.

Now I've done it. They'll never keep me now. Why couldn't I just ignore that cat? Sadly, Wally lay down on the cold, hard tile. Exhausted, he fell asleep.

It was late when Lindsey came to see him in the bathroom. "You've been very naughty, Wally," she said, giving his head a pat. "You have to stay down here tonight, but I'll leave the door open. It's Christmas Eve. Things will be better tomorrow."

He watched as she placed a plate of cookies high up on the mantle. Wally drooled.

"Good night, Wally." Lindsey left him and went upstairs. The cat was in her arms.

Wally's dreams made him restless. He dreamed of Safe Haven and all those dogs laughing when he came back. He dreamed of that cat laughing at him, too, waving his tail in Wally's face.

A thumping on the roof woke him up. The house was dark and everyone was asleep upstairs. Wally heard a scraping sound coming from the living room.

He ventured out from the bathroom to see what it could be. The sound came from the fireplace. Suddenly, something dropped down into the ashes, sending up a cloud of dust.

Wally couldn't believe it. It was a person! He was black with soot, but as he brushed some of it off, a red suit showed through.

"I'm so sorry," the person whispered. "I don't usually make such a clumsy entrance. I'm having a really rough night."

Wally sat very still, his ears at full alert.

"It was foggy over Finland, gusty over Greenland, and sleety over Siberia," the man continued. "Then Blitzen had a tummyache over Thailand. And it doesn't help that these new boots pinch my toes. I didn't have time to break them in."

Wally's tail swept the floor. Shouldn't he bark to let everyone know someone was here? But somehow he trusted the chatty fellow. He watched, fascinated, tilting his head from side to side.

The round little man reached into his sack and pulled out several beautifully wrapped packages. He looked at a tag. "Is there anyone here by the name of Lindsey?"

Wally responded with a tail wag.

"Ah, good. I'm glad to know I'm in the right place. With things going the way they are tonight, one can't be too sure. Oh. Sorry. I'm Santa Claus. And who might you be?"

He reached over to look at Wally's collar. "Hmmm. Your name's not on here." He reached up to the plate of cookies and took a couple. "Lindsey always leaves my favorite — oatmeal raisin." He gave one to Wally and took one himself.

Wally scarfed down the cookie, even the raisins, which he usually left behind, and licked up the crumbs.

Santa Claus brushed the crumbs from his beard and went back to his work. He pulled out a small package wrapped in blue tissue paper. "This is for Mikey," he said.

At the cat's name, Wally whined, lowered himself to the floor, and grunted.

Santa Claus pulled out more presents and placed them around the tree. Wally watched sadly as he realized everyone Santa Claus left gifts for was a part of this family. But Wally's name had not been mentioned.

Santa Claus got up and stretched. "Ah, I feel so much better now," he said. "But before I go, I have one more present to leave. The order came in late, and I had no time to wrap it. It's for someone named Wally. Could that be you?" he asked.

Wally's heart beat faster. A present for him? His ears were so high they almost left his head. His tail thumped wildly.

Santa Claus took out a beautiful green leather collar with a shiny tag hanging from it. He lifted the tag and read it:

WALLY

I BELONG TO LINDSEY
238 CEDAR STREET
201-555-2345

Wally's heart was about to burst out of his chest. He had never had a tag with his name and the name of his person on it before. He had never belonged to anyone long enough.

"Yup," said the jolly man, trying the collar around Wally's neck. "Fits perfectly."

The little man placed the collar under the tree. "Good night, Wally," he said. "Merry Christmas." Then, with a pat and a wink, he climbed back into the chimney and shimmied up.

Wally sighed. It looked like he was home at last. He climbed back onto his bed and went to sleep, dreaming of his shiny new tag.

JIGSAW JONES:
The Case of the Santa Claus Mystery

By James Preller

A Busy Time of Year

Sally Ann Simms was only four years old. Maybe she weighed thirty pounds — if she had rocks in her pocket. Which, come to think of it, was likely. Sally Ann liked rocks. They were fun to bash things with.

Sally Ann Simms was one tough cookie. And in my line of work, I've met a lot of cookies. You see, I'm a detective. Jigsaw Jones, private eye. For a dollar a day, I make problems go away. I've got a partner named Mila

Yeh. Together we've tackled ghosts, found missing falcons, and tracked down stolen bicycles. We've done it all, except for making it past the second grade.

Sally Ann and I were in my basement office. I sat at my desk. Sally Ann sat across from me. She was scowling, staring hard into my eyes. Her arms were crossed. "I want to meet Santa," she demanded.

You could have knocked me down with a wet noodle.

"Santa?" I repeated. "Last name is Claus?"

"That's the one," Sally Ann said.

"Big white beard? Wears black boots and a red suit? Last seen driving a sleigh led by, let's see"— I opened my detective journal and pretended to read —"eight miniature reindeer?"

Sally Ann didn't crack a smile.

Instead, she rummaged inside her pink plastic pocketbook. She pulled out the head of a Barbie doll — that's it, just the head. Sally Ann frowned and continued poking around. She pulled out some baseball cards, a Kleenex (used, I think), and a handful of marbles, jacks, beads, and other assorted junk.

"Here," she finally said.

Sally Ann smoothed out a dollar bill on my desk.

She was serious.

Sally Ann wanted me to help her meet Santa Claus.

And I don't think she was taking no for an answer.

So I thought about Christmas. It was two days away. I still needed to get a present for my Grams. It wasn't going to be much. I had thirty-seven cents left.

There was good old George Washington. The first president of the United States. Just sitting on my desk. Looking lost and lonely. I cannot tell a lie: I stuffed the dollar bill into my pocket.

"It's a deal," I told Sally Ann. "But no promises. Santa is an important guy — and this is his busy time of year."

The Secret Message

That afternoon, I sent Mila a message. In the detective business, you can't be too careful. Spies are everywhere. So we always send our notes in secret code.

I decided to use a color code:

Happy blue we've will the snow ever red got drop green a lions and tigers orange new baseball ooze shoes snooze purple case. Run black I'll zipper flip gray be songs yellow over two more days white soon!

It looks crazy at first. But once you know the trick, it's one of the easiest codes to use. The only words that mattered were the ones that came right after the color words.

All Mila had to do was circle every color word: blue, red, green, and so on. Then she had to underline the words that came next:

We've got a new case. I'll be over soon!

My dog, Rags, was a big slobbering Newfoundland. He had lots of fur. Rags actually *liked* December's deep freeze. I taped the message to his collar and opened the front door. A cold wind slapped my face.

"Go, boy," I ordered. "Go find Mila!"

Rags looked at me as if I were speaking a different language. And I guess I was. But anyway.

I pointed down the block toward Mila's house. "Go on, Ragsy!"

Rags tilted his head. And drooled.

"Deliver the message!" I commanded, then weakly added, "Arf, arf."

Rags curled up on the rug and shut his eyes.

Yeesh.

So I pulled on a sweater, and my winter coat, and hat, and scarf, and gloves. I took the message from my sleepy dog's collar and walked down the block to Mila's house.

Mila was out on her front yard. Get this, she was sitting on a sled. That was strange, since there wasn't any snow on the ground.

She was singing. And like always, Mila made up new words. The song was "Holly Jolly Christmas" — but not the way Mila sang it:

"Build a roly-poly snowman,
It's the best time of the year!"

"What are you doing?" I asked her.

"Positive thinking!" Mila answered cheerfully.

"Huh?"

"I want it to snow, Jigsaw. I want the clouds to open up and drop a gazillion fluffy white snowflakes," Mila said happily. "I want to build snowmen and race in Lincoln Park with my sled. . . ."

"I don't know, Mila," I replied, glancing up at the clear sky. "Snow would be nice, but it doesn't look likely."

"It's not Christmas without snow," Mila protested.

I shrugged. "It's not Halloween, either." I handed the note to her.

Mila rocked back and forth as she read it. That's how Mila got her Thinking Machine started. After a few moments, she broke into a smile.

"Awesome," she cried. "Tell me all about it!"

Setting the Trap

We set the Santa Claus Trap on Christmas Eve.

On the way to Sally Ann's house, Mila was still doubtful. "Why can't we just bring her to the mall like everybody else? Sally Ann can sit on Santa's lap."

"Those are Santa's helpers," I explained. "Sally Ann wants the real deal."

I leaned on the doorbell.

Sally Ann's mom, Mrs. Simms, led us into the living

room. "Sally Ann is waiting for you," Mrs. Simms told us. "What are you kids up to?"

"We're setting a trap for Santa Claus," I replied.

"Oh?"

I shrugged. "It's a living."

Sally Ann was waiting for us beside the Christmas tree. I noticed that the stockings were hung by the chimney with care. Soon, I figured, Santa Claus would be there.

"Here's the plan," I told Sally Ann.

Mrs. Simms sat down on the couch. "You don't mind if I listen, do you?" she asked. "It's so rare that I get to watch real detectives at work."

"No problem," Mila answered.

I continued, "Look, we all know that Santa is a busy guy. Sure, he's magical and all that. But it's got to be rough getting down all these dirty chimneys. He's got to unload the presents, then rush off to nine million other houses."

"It's a tough job," Sally Ann noted.

"Exactly," I agreed. "He's going to be hungry. That will be the bait."

"Bait?" Mrs. Simms echoed nervously.

"Yes, food," I replied.

"We always leave Santa cookies and a glass of milk," Sally Ann said.

I frowned. "Big mistake. Think about it," I said. "Everybody leaves cookies. By the time he gets to your house, Sally Ann, he's probably sick of cookies. I've got a better idea — meat loaf."

"Meat loaf!" Mrs. Simms exclaimed.

"For Santa's reindeer," I explained. "They love the stuff."

Mila pulled a ball of string from her coat pocket. "You should put the meat loaf here," Mila said, pointing to a nearby table. As she spoke, Mila began to wind the string all around the area. Reaching again into her pocket, Mila hung three small bells on the string.

"Cool!" Sally Ann observed.

"When Santa walks toward the meat loaf," I said, "he'll trip the string and ring the bell."

"He could step *over* the string," Mrs. Simms pointed out.

"It'll be dark," I told Mrs. Simms. "Trust me. Santa won't notice the string."

"Gotcha," Sally Ann's mom replied.

"Do you have any crunchy cereal?" Mila asked.

In no time, Sally Ann rushed back with a box of corn flakes. Before I scattered them on the floor, I asked, "You don't have a dog, do you?"

Sally Ann's lips tightened. She glared at her mother, and shook her head, no.

"Cats?"

"No."

"Hamsters, gerbils, fish, orangutans? Any kind of pet at all?" I asked.

No, no, no, no, and no.

Sally Ann didn't seem too happy about it, either.

"Don't feel bad," Mila said to Sally Ann. "A pet could ruin our trap. We're glad you don't have a pet."

"I'm not," Sally Ann scowled. "I don't have a brother. I don't have a sister. I don't even have a crummy goldfish."

"I had a goldfish once," I commented. "It drowned."

Mrs. Simms cleared her throat. "Sally Ann," she warned. "We've been through this before. Please, let's not argue about this on Christmas Eve."

"We should leave," Mila whispered to me.

I quickly tossed some cereal on the floor. "When Santa steps on the floor, it'll make a lot of noise," I explained. "And don't worry about the mess, Mrs. Simms. You can clean it up tomorrow."

The trap was set. I told Mrs. Simms to make really, really tasty meat loaf — "and forget the milk," I instructed. "Santa prefers grape juice."

Mrs. Simms nodded. "Grape juice," she repeated. "Well, I guess I'm cooking meat loaf for Santa."

Sally Ann smiled.

"One last thing," I said. "Sally Ann is going to have to sleep on the couch tonight."

"But . . . ." Mrs. Simms said.

"It's the only way to meet Santa," I explained.

"Please, Mom!" Sally Ann asked.

When please didn't work, Sally Ann shifted to all-out

begging. That did the trick.

"We'll check back tomorrow, on Christmas," I said. "Good luck, Sally Ann."

"Thanks, Jigsaw! Thanks, Mila!" Sally Ann gushed. "I can't wait to meet Santa Claus!"

Snow

I awoke on Christmas morning and the world was white.

Snow had fallen all through the night and all through the day. The snowdrifts grew higher and higher. It snowed as my family opened our gifts. It snowed during breakfast, as we sat around giggling in our new Christmas clothes.

The phone rang and my brother Billy answered it. "It's for you, Worm," he told me.

It was Mila. "Have you looked out your window, Jigsaw? Can you believe it?!"

"You got your snow," I replied. "And plenty of it, too."

The world outside looked like one of those snow globes you shake up — a winter scene filled with white flakes.

"Let's go see how Sally Ann Simms did last night," I said to Mila.

"Bring your sled," Mila reminded me. "We can go to Lincoln Park afterward."

Half an hour later, Mila and I pulled our sleds down the road to Sally Ann's house. Rags came with us.

From a distance we heard, *Yip-yip, yap!* Rags stopped suddenly. He sniffed, lifted his ears, and listened. Then Rags took off in a happy gallop through the falling snow.

Mila and I looked at each other, eyes wide. We raced after Rags . . . and found Sally Ann playing in front of her house . . . with a small black puppy!

Rags and the puppy tussled in the snow.

Sally Ann wore a huge smile on her face. "He came, Jigsaw! He came last night!"

"You mean the trap worked?" I asked. "You saw Santa Claus?"

Sally Ann pulled her hat over her ears. "Not exactly," she said. "But in the middle of the night, I woke up when I heard the cereal crunching. The room was dark. But I think I saw a dark shape, like a body, rush out of the room." Sally Ann smiled. "That's when I got licked."

"Santa licked you?" Mila asked.

"Not Santa." Sally Ann laughed. "My new puppy licked me! Santa brought him."

Mila bent down to pet the puppy. "So who is this little fella?" Mila asked.

"This is Scruffy," Sally Ann said.

"I'm pleased to meet you," Mila said to Scruffy.

"Well, I guess that wraps up this case," I said to Sally Ann. "Are you sure that you are okay with this? You didn't get to meet Santa. That was the deal. We offer a money-back guarantee."

Sally Ann smiled. In fact, she hadn't stopped smiling since we arrived. "I know that Santa's real," Sally Ann said. "He brought me my most secret wish of all — Scruffy."

"That's nice," I said doubtfully. "But it's not proof."

Sally Ann shrugged. "It's proof enough for me. Santa was the only one who knew that I wanted a puppy. I asked for one in a letter. I didn't even tell my parents about it."

Sally Ann paused, "Guess what else? Santa ate the meat loaf!"

I laughed. "Works every time."

"Hey, let's all go to Charlie's Hill," Mila said. "We'll bring the dogs and everything."

"Sure, hop on," I told Sally Ann.

She climbed onto my sled with Scruffy bundled in her arms. Mila walked next to me. Rags raced ahead. I pulled Sally Ann Simms through the snow.

All the way to Charlie's Hill.

Jigsaw Jones, private detective, had decided to take the rest of the day off. After all, it was Christmas!

THE END

THE END

MIDNIGHT GETS A STAR

By Sue Wright

More than two thousand years ago, there lived a stable cat named Midnight. She was perfectly black from paw to paw.

Everyone agreed that Midnight was the finest cat in all of Bethlehem. She lived in the stable of an old inn. Nothing entered Midnight's stable without her permission. No owl perched in the rafters. No bat hung from the eaves. Wasps were not allowed to build a nest in the stable, nor bees a hive. No fly dared buzz the livestock. Midnight scorned spiders and she hated mice.

She hated snakes and toads and lizards, too. She even banned wrens and doves from her stable.

The little cat worked hard all day to keep her master's stable free from "common pests." So by dusk, she enjoyed curling up in her favorite manger for a cat nap. No one seemed to mind. They understood. Midnight needed a rest before nighttime prowls.

One late afternoon, Midnight's tired eyes had barely closed when she heard the innkeeper speaking. He was walking down the path between the stable and the inn.

"It's only a stable, I know," he was saying. "But if you choose to stay the night, I'll send my daughter back with blankets and some food and water."

"Thank you," replied a weary voice. "We'll stay."

Wide awake now, Midnight stretched her back and saw the innkeeper and the two strangers stepping through the door. The little cat felt both curious and disturbed. Why was the innkeeper letting this man and woman and their donkey spend the night in her stable? Since when was a stable for people instead of for cows and horses?

"Shoo!" shouted the innkeeper, distracted by Midnight's rustling in the manger. "Are you spying on us, cat?"

Midnight sprang from the manger and slunk into a dark corner. She was upset that the innkeeper had yelled at her, but she would go no farther. Nothing could make Midnight leave her post.

The little cat was intent on watching her unwanted company. And it was a good thing she did. Almost immediately, astonishing things began to happen.

First, the pretty young woman named Mary gave birth to a baby boy. She and the man called the baby Jesus.

Mary wrapped the baby in soft cloths. She held him close and kissed his face. She touched her cheek to his cheek. She murmured softly to him.

The man, whose name was Joseph, made a crib for the infant from the same manger in which Midnight had been sleeping. Midnight had no way of knowing it, but Joseph was a carpenter. He knew exactly how to rearrange the manger into a comfortable bed.

Midnight had to admit, the baby did look very sweet lying in the manger. "But I don't care how sweet he looks," she grumbled. "He doesn't belong in my stable!" And it was about time she let everybody know.

The trouble was there was so much going on that nobody was paying any attention to Midnight. Too many strangers had begun wandering in and out of the stable. More strangers than the poor cat could count.

First, there was a young shepherd boy, shaggy as his flock, teasing the lamb in his arms. "Look, lamb," he said. "The baby is almost as handsome as you."

The lamb wiggled and went "baa." The boy had made him laugh.

There was a group of older shepherds, too. One of

them was very excited. "I must tell my wife and children the good news," he said. "I want them to see the baby."

In no time, the stable was full of shepherds and their families. Guests from the inn, aroused by all the commotion, also pushed into the stable.

Midnight noticed some of the people were just as confused as she was. They asked the same questions she asked. Who is this baby? What makes him special? Why had three men from far, far away traveled to this stable to bring him gifts?

The three men presented Jesus with gold, perfume, and rare spices. They repeated what the shepherds had said. The baby lying in the manger was the Son of God.

As hard as she was trying not to, even Midnight was beginning to believe what all the people said. Everyone who gazed upon the baby acted different. They seemed happier. They hugged one another. They ran off to tell their neighbors what they had seen.

And there was something else, too. A glowing being had appeared by the child's side.

"It is an angel sent from Heaven," people whispered.

To guard the Baby Jesus, Midnight thought. *Just as I guard the stable!*

But unlike Midnight, the angel wasn't trying to scare anyone away. Quite the opposite. The angel's expression was kind and welcoming. He invited everyone to join in singing praises to the newborn king.

Midnight couldn't help herself. Before she knew it, she was purring praises to the newborn baby in the manger, too.

Then, as abruptly as her beautiful purring had begun, it stopped. In its place came from Midnight's throat the loudest, most pitiful yowl any cat on earth has ever uttered.

"Meow," cried Midnight. "How could I have been so cruel?"

Midnight bounded from her hiding place under the manger and raced into the hills nearby. A star brighter than the brightest moon shone her way.

"Please don't be afraid," she cried into the trees around. "Whoever hears me, I promise, I will never chase you from my stable again. Listen to me, Owl. You must come and see the Baby Jesus. Three wise men and the shepherds say he is the Son of God. Find Bat and Wren and Dove and bring them to the stable."

"Humph," hooted Owl. He didn't know if he could trust the little black cat. In the past, she had brought him and other hillside creatures only harm. Still, she sounded sincere.

"Following this cat is risky," muttered the owl, "but something tells me I should trust her." Spreading his wings, Owl soared off to find Bat, Wren, and Dove.

Meanwhile, Midnight raced into the fields to search out the insects, reptiles, and rodents she had counted as her enemies since kittenhood.

"Listen to me, wasps and bees," she begged. "You must come to the stable and see the Son of God. Invite the flies and spiders and every snake, toad, mouse, and lizard you can. Bring them to the stable. And hurry."

Like their forest kin, the creatures of the fields also decided to give the mean cat another chance.

Midnight had little trouble sneaking her menagerie of new friends in among the human folk bowed before the baby. Quickly, the animals' voices were part of all the other joyful noise that filled the stable.

Owl hooted, and Wren and Dove tweeted and cooed. The insects hummed and buzzed. The reptiles slithered and hissed. The bats and mice began to squeak. Legend has it the spiders were so inspired by the singing they spun a web that turned into silver tinsel.

Then, to everyone's amazement, the angel bade the choir of men and beasts, "Be still."

Once everyone was quiet, the angel began speaking to Midnight.

"Midnight, you aren't still hiding, are you?" the angel asked. "Come stand with me beside the baby."

Midnight was confused. She cowered in the straw beneath the legs of a billy goat.

"Don't be afraid, little kitten," the angel said, laughing. "A heart as changed as yours deserves the Father's blessing!"

Midnight crept to the manger shyly but obediently.

As she did, the magnificent star above the stable beamed down on her. In the blink of an eye, it spread its starry whiteness onto the cat's dark forehead.

Midnight was pure black no longer. From that day forth, a small white star shone on her inky fur. Like everyone else in the stable that Christmas evening, Midnight was forever marked by God's love. And when she began to purr again, all Heaven and Nature joined in her song.

TAKE A PENNY,
LEAVE A PENNY

By Stephanie Calmenson

*Holidays are a time for giving and sharing. In Brook-
lyn, New York, at a time when snacks cost less than
fifty cents, a candy shop owner shares what she can,
even at the risk of being thought a fool.*

"No, Joe!" said Jenny Levy.

"When, Jen?" said her brother, Joe. "When are you
going to figure out that these kids just *take* the pennies?
It's not like they really need them."

"You don't know that," said Jenny. "The penny box

stays. Please. Especially now for the holidays."

Jenny and Joe Levy owned Pop's Candy Shop in the Flatbush section of Brooklyn, New York. The store had been passed down from their mother and father. It was brightly decorated for all the holidays that were celebrated in their neighborhood. In the window was a tree with pretty ornaments for Christmas, a menorah with nine candles for Hanukkah, and a kinara with seven candles for Kwanzaa. These were holidays of giving and sharing.

Though her brother thought she was a fool, Jenny was willing to give to those who didn't need rather than miss the chance to give to someone whose need was real. If it were up to her and she could afford it, the box would be filled with silver dollars!

Jenny pushed the box forward on the counter. Its handwritten sign read, TAKE A PENNY. LEAVE A PENNY.

At school, fourth graders Alan Jasper and Marty Jacobs were watching the clock on their classroom wall. They were tapping their feet with each leap of the second hand: Ten . . . nine . . . eight . . . seven . . . six . . . five . . . four . . . three . . . two . . .

"School's out! Yes!!!" they shouted as the bell rang.

They didn't exactly hate school. They just *loved* when it was over!

The two boys threw on coats, scarves, and hats and burst out of the classroom, pushing aside any kid who got in their way. They weren't exactly bullies. They just *loved* getting where they were going.

They knocked into Dawn Ochobee with her armful of books, spinning her around as they whizzed by. But Dawn was graceful even when a pair of rowdy boys almost ran her down. That's because Dawn was a dancer. Now that school was out, she was heading to her dance class at the Y.

Alan and Marty met up with Roy Johnson. He was tossing a baseball and catching it. No matter where he went or what the season, Roy had that baseball.

"Let's go!" said Marty.

He didn't have to say where. They were heading for Pop's Candy Shop. They went there every day after school to buy candy, soda, pretzels, and comics.

As the three boys walked down the street, Dawn kept her distance. They made her nervous. She wouldn't walk their way if she didn't have to, but the Y was a couple of blocks past Pop's. Dawn hardly ever stopped at the candy shop. Her mom always made an after-school snack for her. It was cheaper than buying food from the store and, for Dawn's family, every penny mattered.

Dawn was glad when her friend Anna Rothman ran to catch up with her.

"Why didn't you wait for me?" asked Anna, out of breath.

"Sorry," said Dawn. "I've got my dance class today."

"Oops! I forgot," said Anna. "I was going to see if you wanted to come over to practice some harmonies."

"How about Saturday?" said Dawn. Dawn loved to sing as much as she loved to dance.

"Saturday's good," said Anna. "My brothers will be home in the morning."

Anna's twin brothers were a couple of years older and really nice. They played backup for Anna and Dawn on guitar and piano.

"Come on, let's do one song now," said Anna.

Dawn's eyes lit up. Her eyes were beautiful. And unusual. One was brown, the other was blue.

"Now you're talking," Dawn said. "What should we sing? 'The Dreidel Song' or 'Jingle Bells'?"

Anna looked at the snow left over from the last storm, then started snapping her fingers and singing, "Dashing through the snow, in a one-horse open sleigh, o'er the fields we go, laughing all the way!"

Her voice was sweet and low. Dawn sang the next lines, her voice rich and strong.

"Bells on bobtail ring, making spirits bright. What fun it is to ride and sing a sleighing song tonight!"

When they joined their voices for the chorus, they sounded like Christmas bells ringing.

"Jingle bells, jingle bells, jingle all the way! Oh, what fun it is to ride in a one-horse open sleigh!"

Dawn pointed to Anna, who sang out, "Jingle bells, jingle bells, jingle all the way!"

Anna pointed back to Dawn just as they reached the corner. Dawn thought fast and sang, "Here we are, I've got to run, I'll see you Saturday!"

Back at Pop's, Jenny was straightening rows of comic books, waiting for the schoolkids to arrive.

"Why do you do that?" asked Joe. "You know the place will be turned upside down as soon as those kids walk in."

"Don't be such a crabapple. You love *those kids* as much as I do," said Jenny.

"I guess," said Joe. "But I know some of them take our pennies when they don't need them. And they make a mess of the place."

"Crab, crab," said Jenny, moving on to straighten a row of candy bars.

"Here they come," said Joe. "I can hear them screaming all the way down the block."

The door burst open, bringing in cold December air and hungry, noisy kids.

"I'm getting a peanut-butter crunch bar and a soda!" said Marty.

"I'm getting pretzels and a comic book," said Roy. "You'll let me have some of your soda, right?"

"Wrong," said Marty. "Get your own."

"Then you can't read my comic book," said Roy.

"Okay, you can have three sips of my soda," said Marty.

"Then you can read three words of my comic!"

While they were bickering, Alan pretended he was reaching for a candy bar, but he swiped a coin from the penny box instead. He turned to show Marty and Roy.

"Go ahead, take one," he whispered. "The sign says you can."

"That's only if you *need* a penny," said Marty. "They're not just handing them out."

"They won't miss a few," said Alan. "If we take one or two every day, we'll have enough for a free candy bar."

"No thanks," said Roy.

"Me, neither," said Marty.

"Then I'll take yours," said Alan.

When Joe and Jenny weren't looking, Alan took two more pennies.

"Cool idea!" whispered Terry, a girl in Alan's computer class, when she saw what he was up to. She reached into the box, grabbed a couple of pennies, and slipped them into her pocket.

Alan and Terry gave each other high fives.

Meanwhile, Dawn was standing outside the candy store. It looked so cheerful with twinkling holiday lights and decorations. But Dawn wasn't feeling one bit cheerful. Her stomach was growling from hunger and she felt like kicking herself. She had left her snack at home on the kitchen table.

Dance class was serious business, and Dawn knew she'd be weak and dizzy if she didn't get something to eat. She figured she had enough pocket money for pretzels and juice, so she went inside.

Dawn picked out a small bag of pretzels and a bottle of apple juice and set them on the counter. Then she started counting out her change. When she realized she was a couple of pennies short, her eyes stung with tears. Jenny looked at those worried eyes, one brown, one blue. She pointed to the penny box.

"Take what you need. That's what it's there for," said Jenny.

Dawn didn't know what to do. She wasn't supposed to just *take* money.

Jenny saw Dawn struggling, so she reached into the penny box, took out two pennies, and added them to Dawn's change. She put the pretzels and juice in a bag, then reached into the box for one more penny — a shiny, new one — and pressed it into Dawn's palm.

"That's for good luck," she said. "Come again soon. And happy holidays!"

Dawn thanked her and hurried out.

Racing to get to class, Dawn wolfed down her snack and had just enough time to get into her dance clothes.

"Deep breaths," she told herself as she took her place. "Deep breaths."

The instructor began with the usual warm-up

stretches, then continued with the routine they had been working on the week before. The dance began slowly and Dawn moved like liquid, getting lost in the rhythm and movements. Then drums began to beat, faster and faster, as she and her classmates flew across the room, heads tossed back, arms spread wide, leaping and twirling.

When the class ended, Dawn was drenched in sweat and almost giddy with the joy of doing what she loved most. She felt she had done well, considering what a mess she'd been when class had started.

It wasn't unusual for people to come watch the class — friends, relatives, student teachers — so Dawn hadn't thought twice when she saw a man and woman sitting at the back of the room. Now they were point- ing in her direction; her teacher was calling her name. Dawn had no idea what this could be about. She wiped her hands and face with her towel and went to meet them.

Ten years later . . .
Dawn's life changed that day ten years ago. The two visitors to her class were directors from the top music and arts programs in Manhattan. They chose Dawn to attend their school on a scholarship. Along with the opportunity to study came opportunities to perform.

The parts started out small and stayed small for years. A spot on a TV commercial. A part in an off-off-

Broadway play. Then Dawn's life changed once again. She landed a leading role on the TV series *Rhythm and Blues*, about three friends trying to make it as singers and dancers in New York City. The show took off.

When Dawn started earning money, her family was able to move to Manhattan so she could be closer to school and work. Dawn and Anna still managed to see each other sometimes, but mostly in Manhattan. Dawn and her family missed Brooklyn, but they didn't have much time to go back. So when an invitation came for her to speak at her elementary school, Dawn jumped at the chance. She wanted to talk to kids and tell them how a life can change. And there was someone else in Brooklyn she wanted to see.

As Dawn stood in front of Pop's Candy Shop, she felt as though she'd been magically transported back in time. It was mid-December and, once again, the shop was decorated with twinkling holiday lights and decorations. The shop was a little run-down and, peeking inside, Dawn could see that Jenny and Joe looked quite a bit older. Dawn was just glad they were there. It was Jenny she wanted to see.

There were bells over the door now and they rang as Dawn walked inside.

Jenny and Joe weren't the only ones in the shop. Alan Jasper was there, too, straightening up shelves and stacking candy bars. Joe had caught him stealing pennies one day and asked him to work at the shop to pay back all the pennies he'd taken. Now Alan was working at the shop for pay, to help put himself through college.

Though Dawn and Alan had hardly spoken when they were in school, Alan recognized Dawn right away.

"Wow. What brings you back to Brooklyn?" he asked. "You're pretty famous these days."

"I was invited to talk to kids at our old school. And I wanted to see Jenny," said Dawn.

Jenny did not recognize Dawn at first. She had only met her that once, and Jenny didn't watch much TV. But when Dawn walked up to the counter and Jenny looked into her eyes, one brown, one blue, she remembered. The only difference was that instead of being worried and tear-filled, Dawn's eyes were warm and proud.

"You once gave me two pennies so I could buy a snack," said Dawn.

She took two pennies from her wallet and put them in the penny box.

"You gave me another penny for good luck," she said.

She took that very same penny, no longer shiny, out of a silk pouch.

Jenny smiled. "I remember," she said. "It's good to see you again."

Dawn told her what happened that day ten years ago.

"It's taken me way too long, but I came to thank

you," she said.

Now it was Jenny's eyes that were filled with tears.

"Will you come see a taping of my show some-time?" asked Dawn. "It would mean a lot to me." She held out two tickets.

"We'll be there," said Jenny. "Thank you for coming back."

"Thank *you*," said Dawn. "For more than I can say."

Dawn bought a bag of pretzels and an apple juice, then headed out to tell some kids her story.

When she left, Joe turned to Jenny and said, "I guess you weren't such a fool with that penny box after all."

"No, I don't think so," said Jenny. "The look I saw in those eyes was worth all the pennies in the world."

She opened the cash register, took out a handful of pennies, and filled the penny box to the top.

"Happy holidays," she said.

THE NUTCRACKER RETOLD

By Sue Wright

"Mother," Clara cried, "Fritz has untied the bow on my dress again. Make him stop."

Their mother frowned. "Fritz," she said in her sternest voice, "leave your sister alone. Why must you be so naughty? Be good now. Our guests will be here any moment. Wipe the cookie from your mouth and go help your father trim the tree."

Fritz grinned wildly and gave the bow on his sister's dress another mischievous tug. Luckily for her, someone was knocking at the door.

"They're here!" shouted Fritz. "Everyone is here."

"They are indeed," the children's father said.

All at once, the house was filled with people dressed in their finest holiday clothes. The men wore tuxedos; the women long gowns and dangling earrings. Everyone greeted one another with cries of "Merry Christmas!" There were hugs all around.

While the grown-ups drank punch and sampled platefuls of Christmas goodies, the children gathered around the Christmas tree to admire the packages. They played tag, London Bridge, and leap frog.

Boys chased girls and girls chased boys. And everybody — including the adults — chased Fritz.

When the ladies and gentlemen began to dance, the children stopped what they were doing to join in. The boys practiced their bows. The girls practiced their curtsies. Shiny patent leather slippers met polished boots and skipped away.

At the stroke of ten, Clara's father silenced the orchestra. "It's present time!" he announced.

Instantly, the children gathered around him in a circle, their faces eager with anticipation.

"I hope I get a doll," said Clara and Fritz's cousin Amy. She crossed her fingers on both hands.

"Dolls are stupid!" responded her brother Max. "I want a drum."

Not a child was disappointed. Max got the drum he had wished for. The other boys received bright balls, building blocks, and toy trumpets. Each girl received a baby doll wearing a lace dress and velvet booties.

Clara was happy with her doll. Still, she looked forward to the Christmas present her godfather, Drosselmeier, would be bringing. The toy maker was magical, and so were his gifts.

"I wonder where he is," Clara whispered aloud. And then, like magic, her godfather appeared.

"Godfather!" Clara exclaimed. "I thought you'd never get here. Where have you been?"

Drosselmeier didn't answer. He was too busy introducing his young nephew to the crowd.

It was hard to believe the man and the boy could be related. Drosselmeier was cloaked in black from the top hat on his head to the points of his shoes. Even the patch on his bad eye was black. He looked very mysterious — almost frightening. But his nephew was as handsome as any boy Clara had ever seen.

Once the introductions were made, the children surrounded Drosselmeier eagerly. "Show us a magic trick," they begged.

"My pleasure," he replied grandly. As always, Drosselmeier had come to the party prepared. The toy maker carried three boxes with him. On his command, the toys in these boxes began to move. The dolls twirled on their toes. The band marched to its own music. Everyone gasped in amazement.

Clara watched the marvelous toys. She couldn't wait to see what her godfather had brought for her.

And she would not have to wait long. In two blinks of an eye, Clara was holding a miniature hobbyhorse. The girl shrieked with delight.

"Oh, thank you, Godfather," Clara said. "It's the best toy ever."

"Let me see," her brother, Fritz, demanded. He was jealous of his sister's remarkable toy. He snatched it away and raced off to show his friends.

Clara began to cry.

"No matter, my darling girl," Drosselmeier reassured her. "I have something even better." And from out of nowhere, he pulled a Nutcracker in the shape of a toy soldier.

Clara looked puzzled at what the object might be. So her godfather showed her how the Nutcracker opened a nut. Then he passed the toy soldier back to the girl. Her face shone with happiness.

"I love the Nutcracker," Clara whispered in her god-father's ear.

Unfortunately, Fritz had seen Herr Drosselmeier give Clara the second present, and he was more jealous than ever. Without asking, Fritz yanked the Nut-cracker from Clara's hands and began whipping it through the air. Before anyone could stop him, the boy had let the Nutcracker fly. It fell to the floor with a loud crack.

Her cheeks wet with tears, Clara knelt beside the toy soldier. "My poor dear Nutcracker," she sobbed.

The girl's heart was as broken as the Nutcracker.

Herr Drosselmeier's nephew searched for a way to comfort the lovely young girl.

"Ah, here is what she needs," he said. Beneath the Christmas tree was a new doll bed. He offered it to the sorrowful girl, suggesting she wrap the Nutcracker in a blanket and let him rest.

"Now, dry your eyes," he said, "and come dance with me."

Clara couldn't resist. She set the Nutcracker aside and spent what was left of the evening dancing with her godfather's handsome nephew.

The party ended shortly after midnight. A tired but happy Clara yawned and climbed into bed.

Moments later, she was sound asleep, dreaming of her godfather, his nephew, and the Nutcracker. Then she dreamed her brother was stealing the Nutcracker again, and she awoke with a start.

"How could I be so thoughtless?" she asked. "My broken Nutcracker is downstairs all by himself."

Clara found the Nutcracker where she had left him in the parlor. She cradled the Nutcracker in her arms. Then, too weary to go back upstairs, she curled up on the sofa beside the Christmas tree and fell asleep.

Clara's mother spied her daughter sleeping next to the tree. She smiled at her daughter, covered her with a shawl, and tiptoed out of the room.

No sooner was Clara's mother gone from the room than a shadowy figure appeared. It was the toy maker, Drosselmeier. He had slipped back into the house. He was hunting for something. The Nutcracker!

He found the little soldier tucked under Clara's arm. Drosselmeier pulled him away from her ever so gently. Then he repaired the Nutcracker with a magic spell and returned him to the girl.

Despite her godfather's careful movements, Clara heard something stirring. She sat up and rubbed her eyes. Was she awake or asleep? Clara wasn't sure. But it didn't matter. For there were mysterious things happening all around. The Christmas tree was growing taller and taller. And it wasn't just the tree. Everything in the room was getting bigger, including a gang of mice and their horrible Mouse King! The mice were fighting Fritz's toy army, which had also grown bigger — and come to life.

It didn't take long for Clara to understand. She was the reason for the fighting. The Mouse King planned to carry Clara off and make her his queen.

"I'll never go with you!" she screamed at the giant mouse. "Not in a thousand years."

"Don't be afraid," spoke a reassuring voice beside her. "I will protect you."

Clara couldn't believe her eyes. It was the Nutcracker. He had become a life-size prince. And he looked just like Drosselmeier's nephew.

"She's mine, not yours," yelled the Mouse King. And he began to swipe at the prince with his sword.

In no time, the room was gripped in a terrible battle. Though the prince and the toy army fought bravely, it looked as though the Mouse King was winning.

Desperate to help the prince, Clara pulled off her slipper and threw it at the Mouse King. It hit him with a *splat*, and to everyone's shock, the Mouse King tumbled over. He was dead.

"You've defeated him!" the prince said. "Hooray for Clara!" He took the crown from the Mouse King's head. Bowing low, he presented it to the girl.

"My princess," he said softly. "As your reward, I shall take you on a trip you will never forget."

In a flash, Clara and the prince were flying through the window on the Nutcracker's toy bed.

"But where are we going?" Clara asked.

"To the Kingdom of Sweets and Waltzing Flowers," the prince explained gaily. "The Sugar Plum Fairy will show us sights and sounds beyond anything you could ever imagine. Hold on, we're almost there."

And smooth as silk, they landed in the middle of a forest iced with silver frost.

Giant snowflakes and gold-winged angels swept about the boy and girl. And then, suddenly, they were face-to-face with the Sugar Plum Fairy. The fairy extended one hand in welcome and waved a magic wand with the other.

"Oh, my," Clara sighed. "I think I shall faint."

"No time for that," said the Sugar Plum Fairy, laughing. "Look! The dancing has begun."

And so it had.

From the Sugar Plum Fairy's throne, Clara and the prince watched troupes of costumed dancers pirouette and jump through the air from every direction. It was the most amazing performance Clara had ever seen.

As a final treat, the Sugar Plum Fairy cavorted in a graceful duet with her cavalier. She swirled faster than the wind, and he leaped as high as a deer.

When they were done, the Sugar Plum Fairy turned to Clara. "My dear, the hour has come to bid you and your prince farewell."

And without another word, a sleigh floated from the clouds to whisk the girl and boy away.

When Clara awoke on Christmas morning, there was no sign of the prince or the Kingdom of Sweets and Waltzing Flowers. All was not lost to the girl, however. The toy maker's goddaughter never forgot her beautiful dream. And she always treasured the Nutcracker that was nestled in her arms.

HOLIDAY DISASTER

By Debbie Dadey and Marcia Thornton Jones

"Not so hard," Mrs. Malcolm told Angela.

Mrs. Malcolm was too late. Angela pounded the hammer just like she thought a real elf would. Hard.

C-R-A-C-K! The table wobbled. It swayed. The legs buckled and the table crashed to the floor, spilling toys all over the stage.

The rest of the third graders giggled. Angela's face turned bright red. "Sorry," she mumbled.

Angela wanted to be a perfect elf for the third-grade play. So far, the only thing she had done was make a perfect fool of herself. She walked quickly behind the thick purple curtain. She didn't want anyone to see her.

"Reindeer don't giggle!" their teacher said, clapping her hands to get the rest of the students' attention. The kids who were pretending to be reindeer stood in the center of the stage, rehearsing their lines.

Billy edged up beside Angela and whispered, "Why'd Mrs. Malcolm choose you to be the head elf? She should know by now that everything you touch turns to mush."

His words stung worse than ice on a cold winter's day. Angela was wondering the exact same thing. Of course, she couldn't let Billy know that. Billy was an expert at one thing: pestering people.

"Go away," Angela snapped. She stomped her elf shoe so he'd know she meant business.

Billy stayed right where he was. "I'd be much better as Santa's lead toy maker. After all, everyone knows the best elves are boys. This play is going to be one big holiday disaster all because of you!"

Angela was afraid that Billy was right, but that didn't stop her from wanting to sock him in the nose. She didn't, though, because she was pretty sure head elves weren't supposed to hit other elves.

"You always pick on me," Angela said. "And I've had it!"

Billy put his hands on his hips and spoke in a high voice. "I've had it," he mocked. "Like, I'm SO scared of a misfit elf!"

Billy stepped in front of Angela to watch the reindeer, blocking Angela's view.

Angela wasn't just mad. She was furious. She took off her elf cap to whack Billy over the head. At least that's what she meant to do. The cap flew out of her hands and missed Billy completely. It sailed over his head and landed right in front of the tiniest reindeer of them all. Sally.

Sally jumped back and screamed, which Angela thought was silly. After all, reindeer don't scream. That wasn't the worst of it.

When Sally jumped, she bumped into a ladder. The ladder crashed to the floor right where the art teacher was painting the backdrop for Santa's North Pole toy shop. The paint tray tipped over and puddles of colored paint poured across Mr. Buckner's shoes.

Mr. Buckner hopped away from the paint.

The reindeer didn't giggle this time as Mrs. Malcolm rushed over to help him. They laughed out loud.

"I'm sorry," Angela mumbled. "I'm really sorry."

Billy shook his head at Angela and whispered, "What did I tell you? A total disaster!"

Angela felt her face burn redder than ever. She was sure it matched Rudolph's nose. She hated the way every third grader stared at her as if she, Angela Michaels, was sure to ruin their holiday play.

Mr. Buckner called after her. Mrs. Malcolm tried to block her way, but Angela was too fast. She dodged around the teachers and ran across the cafeteria. She headed straight to her favorite place in the whole school — a giant old bathtub filled with pillows in the corner of her classroom.

When Angela climbed inside the tub, her curled elf shoe got caught in the green-and-red garland Mrs. Malcolm had hung around the edge. It ripped in two with a loud *CRACK*.

Nothing was going right. Absolutely nothing.

Angela was still in the tub when Katisha found her. Katisha was dressed as a Christmas tree. It was the perfect part for her because she was the tallest kid in third grade. She was also Angela's best friend.

When Katisha sat down, all the ornaments on her Christmas tree costume clinked together. "Why'd you run away?" Katisha asked.

Angela slid lower in the tub. "Billy is right. I mess up everything. I can't be in our play. I can't."

Katisha shook her head, and the star on top of her hat swayed. "What you can't do is listen to Billy. He's nothing but hot air."

"I just destroyed the set," Angela said. "I can't walk across the stage without tripping. I just can't."

Katisha shook her head and the star wiggled back and forth. "You run up and down a soccer field and don't have any problems. In fact, you're the best player on the team. Walking across the stage should be as easy as kicking a soccer ball for you."

"But I have pages and pages of lines to learn," Angela told her best friend. "I've never been good at remembering things. I can't even remember how much eight times seven is! Not like you. You remember everything. Mrs. Malcolm should have picked you. I'll never remember all those lines. Never."

Katisha laughed, and the jingle bells on her costume rang merrily. "My voice isn't loud enough," she said, "but you can make your voice heard all the way across the cafeteria. I know you can learn the lines if you practice. Mrs. Malcolm must have thought you could. That's why she chose you for the biggest part."

"But the play is only four days away!" Angela moaned. "And that's not the worst part."

Katisha's eyes got big. "There's something else?"

Angela's face grew so pale she blended in with the bathtub. "Every time I think about standing in front of all those people, I have a strange feeling in the middle of my stomach. It's as if I've eaten too many sugar cookies."

Katisha laughed again. "That's just nerves," she said. "You'll be fine."

"You don't understand," Angela said sadly. "This play has to be perfect because my dad is coming all the way from New York just to see me. It's the first time my mom and dad have been in the same room since they got a divorce. What if I mess up? What if I trip over my elf shoes? What if I get sick in front of everyone?

My dad will be so embarrassed he won't want to spend Christmas with me ever again. I'll absolutely ruin Christmas!"

"You can't ruin Christmas," Katisha said. "Your mom and dad won't care one bit if you mess up because they aren't coming to see the play. They're coming to see YOU."

"Do you really think so?" Angela asked. "Do you really think I can do this?"

"Yep," Katisha said. "I know you can. What we CAN'T do is let Billy be right. So quit worrying and let's go back to practice."

Katisha helped Angela out of the tub. Then the two of them retaped the garland around the edge.

When Angela got back to the cafeteria, she went right up to Mr. Buckner. "I'm sorry about your shoes," she said.

The kids on the stage grew quiet. They waited to see if Mr. Buckner would get mad.

Mr. Buckner looked down at his shoes. Then he looked at Angela. "Are you kidding?" he asked. "I LOVE these shoes! Just look at how the colors blend. These are the best shoes I've ever seen!"

Angela couldn't help but smile just a little. Maybe things wouldn't be so bad after all.

Angela worked on her lines for the rest of the week. Katisha helped her. Each day it got a little easier to remember all the words. Finally, the day of the play arrived. Angela was dressed in her elf costume. Katisha was decorated as the best tree ever.

As soon as Billy arrived backstage, he marched right up to Angela. "You'd better not mess up our play," he warned.

"You'd better get your finger away from my nose," Angela told him.

Billy shook his head. "I still can't believe YOU get to be the head elf," he said. "This is SO wrong."

Angela didn't have time to worry about Billy. Mr. Buckner ushered the kids to their places. Mrs. Malcolm played the opening song on the piano. The thick heavy curtain went up, and Angela gasped.

Spotlights sparkled on a wintry scene complete with a giant snowman. "It's perfect," Angela whispered.

And then the play started.

Angela's stomach fluttered when the reindeer pranced on the stage. Her stomach absolutely flopped when it was time for the elves to make their entrance.

"I can't do this," Angela whispered. "I can't. I can't. I can't."

Katisha was right behind her. "Yes, you can," she whispered back. "Besides, you don't have a choice."

It was true. Mrs. Malcolm had already played the opening lines of the song three times. Everybody was waiting for Angela go to center stage.

"Hurry up before you really blow it," Billy said.

Angela took a deep breath and stepped onto the

stage. She walked to the middle just like she had practiced. The cafeteria was packed with people looking at her. Right in the front row sat her father. Her mother was in the row behind him. Angela gulped. She swallowed. She was afraid she would mess up. Finally, she realized that if she didn't say anything, the play really *would* be ruined.

"I can do this," Angela mumbled. "I can."

Angela took a deep breath and said her lines. Perfectly.

She had done it! Angela turned and grinned at Billy when it was his turn.

Billy didn't see her. He was staring at the audience.

"Go on," Angela hissed. "It's your turn."

Billy blinked.

"What's wrong?" Angela whispered.

Billy opened his mouth, but no words came out. He looked like a giant fish staring out of a glass bowl. His face was as white as the fake snow on the stage.

Angela knew exactly what was wrong. For once in his life, Billy was scared speechless.

"Do something," Mrs. Malcolm whispered from behind the piano. A few of the reindeer giggled.

Angela held her hand to Billy's forehead as if taking his temperature. "Dear me," she said in her loudest acting voice. "I do believe the helper elf sang so many Christmas songs he lost his voice. It's off to the nurse elf with you!"

The audience clapped as Angela led Billy to the side

of the stage.

"Quick thinking," Mr. Buckner told her as he helped Billy to a seat. "But who's going to say Billy's lines?"

Angela had been practicing all week. She knew just what to do. "Don't worry," she whispered. "The show must go on!"

And it did. Billy had been wrong. The play hadn't been a disaster.

Angela remembered every one of her lines — and every one of Billy's lines, too. Well, almost every one.

At the end of the play, Angela was supposed to say, "And that's the end of another perfect holiday at Santa's toy shop." But that's not what came out.

Angela waited for the reindeer to finish their song and hoof-dance before stepping up to the microphone. She used her loudest acting voice to say, "And that's the end of another holiday disaster!"

Laughter rang throughout the audience. Angela's hand flew to her mouth. Had she really said that?

Tears welled in her eyes — until she saw her mom and dad. They both stood up and clapped as hard as they could. Angela hadn't been perfect, and it didn't matter one bit to her mom and dad. Her family loved her even when she messed up.

In fact, the entire audience clapped and cheered. She wiped the tears from her eyes and smiled. She'd done a good job, and she was proud of herself for trying. Angela knew, then and there, that celebrating

‎stmas wasn't about being perfect. It wasn't even
‎ disasters. It was about families, friendship, and
‎happiness.

I can have a perfect holiday, Angela thought as she bowed. *I CAN!*

CHRISTMAS ON THE PRAIRIE

By Sue Wright

"Dust, dust, dust," grumbled Katy. "All we do is dust, dust, dust!"

Stella smiled at her grumpy little sister. "Oh, Katy, stop complaining. Just be glad we finally have a real home."

"A house made of dirt is not a real home, Stella. Real homes are made of wood and brick. Like Nana and Grandfather's."

"Katy, our house isn't made of dirt and you know it! It's made of sod."

Katy turned up her nose but kept on dusting. She didn't really mind the daily dusting. She didn't even mind her family's new house. She just missed St. Louis.

She missed living in her grandparents' fine home there. And she missed the yellow daisies on the wallpaper in the bedroom she and her sister had shared.

Katy wondered to this day why their father had moved them to Nebraska. He had been the boss of Grandfather's sawmill. Why decide to be a farmer? But over a year ago, Jim Billings had moved out west and staked a claim for a new farm.

Then, six months ago, the girls' mother had received a letter from him. He said their new sod house was ready. Within the week, he and the girls' older brother, Ben, would be in St. Louis. They would load the family's belongings into a covered wagon. Ten days later, they moved into their "soddy" home.

Building the sod house had been hard work. First, Mr. Billings and Ben had to plow an acre of the Billings' new prairie farmland into strips. Each soil strip was twelve inches wide and four inches thick. These strips were cut into three-foot-long sod bricks. After that, they were piled into walls, two feet deep.

Ben told his sisters the sod was always laid grass-side down. "We soddy owners call the sod bricks 'Nebraska marble,'" he added proudly.

Once the windows and door were in place, Ben and his father forced rags and grass into any cracks left in the walls. They added log rafters and a roof. The roof was made of berry bushes and more sod.

A stove was set in the dirt floor to keep the family warm when winter came. Jim and his son stored away weeds, straw, and cornstalks to use as fuel.

To finish the soddy, Mr. Billings tacked white muslin cloth to the ceiling. He had heard the cloth would catch the extra soil, mice, and bugs that often fell during heavy rainstorms.

Katy had never been more scared than she was traveling in the wagon for a week from Missouri to Nebraska. Twice, the wagon got stuck in a rut. Twice, a big wind almost tipped it over. A snake shook its rattler at Katy. And worst of all, the pack mule took a bite of her ponytail.

During lunch their first day on the trail, the girls' father had laughed at the fancy sandwiches Nana had sent along for their trip. Katy wasn't sure, but she suspected the fancy sandwiches were part of the reason Mr. Billings was taking his family to Nebraska. Her father wasn't like Katy. Mr. Billings hated fancy things.

"Remember Nana's cucumber sandwiches?" Katy asked her sister dreamily.

"How could I forget them?" Stella answered, licking her lips. "They were so good. I wonder if she'll serve them on Christmas Eve again this year."

"Don't even mention Christmas," Katy pleaded, tears welling in her eyes.

Stella pulled a clean dust rag from her apron and

dabbed Katy's tears away. "Why are you crying, Sis?" she asked.

"Nana and Grandfather's house was so pretty at Christmas, and ours will be so ugly!" Katy cried.

"No it won't," promised Stella. "Now hush. If Mother sees you crying, she may start crying, too. You aren't the only one who's homesick, Katy. All of us are, just a little. Quit being a ninny, and I'll tell you a secret."

"Like what?"

"Like how we're going to decorate for Christmas. I have all kinds of ideas. Mother, too. We're even going to have a party. Mother asked Father if we could, and he said, 'Why not?' "

"A party — with cucumber sandwiches?" asked Katy hopefully.

"I'm afraid not. No cucumber sandwiches. But there will be lots of other delicious things to eat. Keep dusting and I'll tell you."

Stella thought their Christmas decorating should begin with hanging paper snowflakes from the muslin cloth ceiling. "Do you remember making snowflakes in school last year?" she asked Katy.

"I remember," Katy answered. "But what will we do for white paper?"

"Mother says we can have the newspaper Nana sent her in the mail."

"Mama's only newspaper?"

"She says she doesn't mind, if we don't mind black-and-white snowflakes."

Katy had to admit the snowflakes turned out quite lovely. Mrs. Billings poked each snowflake through with a needle and thread and stitched it into the ceiling. Though Mr. Billings and Ben made a great to-do about ducking under the snowflakes, they had to agree that the decorations looked wonderful.

Katy blew at a snowflake and watched it flutter. "I never dreamed a sod house could look this Christ-massy," she said.

The snowflakes were only the beginning. A few days later, Mrs. Billings surprised her daughters with a roll of red-and-green-plaid ribbon. She said Nana must have hidden it in a box when nobody was looking.

The girls cut the ribbon into sections. After putting two pieces of the ribbon aside, they tied the rest into bows all around the soddy. They tied bows on the backs of chairs, around candlesticks — everywhere. They even attached one to Ben's hat where it hung on a peg.

When he saw the hat, Ben started a fuss. "Mother," he yelled, "make them stop. The girls have gone ribbon-crazy!"

To prevent an all-out war, Mrs. Billings sent her son outside to do a favor for her. She asked Ben to collect any bits of greenery he could find. She knew there wouldn't be much. The prairie was mostly brown now — or white with snow.

What Ben found, his mother praised. There were

nuts, wild holly, and boughs of cedar. She arranged the odds and ends into a bouquet for the kitchen table. A piece of ribbon was perched in the middle.

A week before Christmas, Mr. Billings and his children bundled up and hiked to the woods near their house. It was there they found a Christmas tree. Ben complained it looked more like a Christmas shrub than a Christmas tree, but the girls and their father were certain it would do.

"Mother said it can't be too big," Katy reminded her brother. "She isn't even sure where we'll put a tree as small as this one."

The Billings had brought a few Christmas tree ornaments from St. Louis, but not many. When they were hung and the last piece of ribbon tied on the tree as a topknot, Katy looked at Stella and frowned.

"Our tree is so bare," she said.

"Close your eyes and we'll see if I can fix that." It was Mr. Billings speaking. "All of you close your eyes," he said. "And no peeking."

Everyone closed their eyes. A minute later Mr. Billings shouted, "You can open them!"

"More Christmas ornaments," Katy sang out. "But where did they come from?"

"Believe it or not, Katy, your old father carved them while you and Stella and your mother were still in Missouri. I even carved a manger scene. If it suits your mother, we'll set it on the organ."

When she saw the Baby Jesus and the Mary and Joseph her husband had carved, Mrs. Billings burst into tears. Not sad tears — happy ones. Mrs. Billings was feeling very blessed. And she already felt more blessed than most of her neighbors. Why? Because the Billings were the only family for miles around who had an organ in their soddy.

Getting the organ shipped to Nebraska had been no easy task, but anyone who heard Mrs. Billings play knew it was worth the effort. At night she performed concerts for her children and their father. Since November, she had been practicing Christmas carols.

The whole family — even Mr. Billings — was looking forward to the Billingses' Christmas party. If the weather didn't blow in a blizzard, the neighbors would arrive at about three o'clock on Christmas Eve. They would sing carols around the organ and taste one another's holiday baking. They would exchange handcrafted gifts. There was much to celebrate this year of 1873. Nebraska had finally declared December twenty-fifth an official state holiday.

Early Christmas Eve morning, Stella perched herself on one of the soddy's windowsills. It was her favorite seat in the house.

"Please, God," she prayed, "don't let it snow and ruin our party. You can let it snow all you want tomorrow and the next day, but not today."

Katy pushed in beside her sister. She had been praying the same prayer herself. Then she giggled and turned to her sister.

"Stella, remember the time we sat here while Mother played the organ, and all of a sudden, those Pawnee boys were staring through the window at us. You screamed and I screamed and then the boys screamed."

Stella sighed. "I'm glad they weren't so scared they didn't come back."

Since that evening, the three Native American boys had stood at the Billingses' window on many occasions. They seemed to enjoy listening to Mrs. Billings play the organ. One night, Mr. Billings asked them if they wanted to come inside to hear the music better.

One of the boys ran away, but the other two followed Jim Billings into the soddy. When Mrs. Billings finished the song she was playing, she greeted the youngsters and motioned them to come closer.

"Press here," she said, showing them what to do.

Cautiously, each boy pressed one of the keys and grew amazed at the grand sound he made. But neither boy had come into the house again.

By two o'clock Christmas Eve, the sun was still shining brightly. Not a single snowflake floated from the sky.

The girls and their brother and mother scurried about in last-minute tidying up. Then they began discussing where they would fit their guests. Four families were expected, a total of fifteen people.

Ben looked grim. "There's no way we can fit us and fifteen more people in this little house," he said.

Stella stuck out her tongue. "You're supposed to help us, not complain!"

Ben didn't respond to his sister until her back was turned. Then he yanked her pigtails as hard as he could.

"Ouch," Stella cried. "If it wasn't Christmas Eve, Ben Billings, I'd chase you down and box your ears. I hope Santa is watching and doesn't leave you even the tiniest thing under the tree."

Ben rolled his eyes, but told his sister he was sorry. It wasn't worth making Santa mad. Like his younger sisters, Ben was counting on Santa Claus to leave him at least one present under the tree. He'd been telling everybody for a month he needed a new pocketknife.

Mrs. Billings put her arms around her son. "Don't forget," she said, "Christmas is the season of miracles. Our home is small, Ben, but somehow there will be room for everyone."

And somehow there was. In less than an hour, the soddy was alive with singing. Folks ate and sang and opened Christmas packages.

With no sign of bad weather, the festivities continued well into the evening. Nobody noticed how dark it had become in the soddy. Why would they? There was such a glow of good cheer.

It was in that spirit that Mr. Billings gathered his

neighbors around the organ for one more verse of "Silent Night." No one noticed the three Pawnee boys listening at the window. No one except Stella, who happened to glance in their direction. Tugging at her father's sleeve, she pointed toward the boys.

Mr. Billings moved to the door and opened it wide. "Come in," he said.

The three boys stepped through the crowd of strangers and stood before Mrs. Billings and the organ.

"Merry Christmas," Mrs. Billings said.

Each boy pulled something from the leather pouch he carried on his back. "For you," they said, handing Mrs. Billings their gifts: a tom-tom, a gourd shaker, and a reed flute painted red.

"Thank you!" breathed Mrs. Billings, looking at the gifts with delight.

The boys nodded and started for the door.

"Wait," Mr. Billings called. "We have something for you, too."

And with that, he untied three of the ornaments he had carved — a star, a bell, and a feather.

"Please," he begged. "Take these."

Even years later, when she had a fancy home in St. Louis and could serve Nana's cucumber sandwiches whenever she wanted, Katy swore she never enjoyed a finer Christmas than her family's first Christmas on the prairie.

HORRIBLE HARRY
READER'S THEATER

The Rocking Chair:
A Classroom Play

By Suzy Kline

From *Horrible Harry and the Christmas Surprise*

Cast of Players

Harry	Sidney	Narrator
Doug	Song Lee	SFX (sound effects person)
Miss Mackle	Ida	Props Manager
Mary	Mr. Cardini	ALL

Setting: The Classroom
Time: December morning
Props: 3 wooden kindergarten blocks
1 empty metal wastepaper basket

SFX: *Krikkity krikk! Krikkity krekk!*

NARRATOR: The teacher rocked back and forth in her old rocking chair. Harry leaned forward, opening his mouth to speak.

HARRY: (*Makes a toothy smile.*) Don't you love that creaky old rocking chair, Doug?

DOUG: Not really. (*To the audience.*) But Harry does. He loves things like that . . . creepy things, slimy things, and horrible sounds. I know. I sit next to him in Room 2B. Harry's my best friend.

MARY: (*To the audience.*) Harry's cat even has a creepy name — Googer. (*Mary shivers.*) Sometimes he calls him "the Goog."

NARRATOR: Suddenly, a fire engine zoomed by South School.

SFX: *DEE-doo! DEE-doo! DEE-doo!*

NARRATOR: Harry jumped out of his seat and ran to the window.

HARRY: (*Stands up and runs in place.*) Neat-o! There it goes! Cool!

SFX: *DEE-doo! DEE-doo! DEE-doo!*

HARRY: Look at that fire truck rev up the hill!

SFX: *Vroom . . . vroom . . . VROOM!*

MISS MACKLE: Harry? I'm waiting. . . .

HARRY: (*Reluctantly.*) Yes . . . Miss Mackle. (*Sits down.*)

MISS MACKLE: Now that we're all in our seats, it's time for a story. It's a holiday classic that has been read over and over for almost two hundred years.

ALL: Two hundred years?

SIDNEY: (*Throws his hands in the air.*) Why read a story if everyone has read it before?

MISS MACKLE: Because it's soooo good, Sidney.

SIDNEY: I'm plugging my ears. (*Plugs ears.*)

ALL: READ THE STORY!

SONG LEE: Please.

NARRATOR: Miss Mackle opened up her big, heavy storybook.

MISS MACKLE: It's called "A Visit from St. Nicholas" by Clement C. Moore.

MARY: I love that story!

SIDNEY: (*Unplugging his ears.*) Me, too!

ALL: (*Clap and cheer.*)

IDA: Miss Mackle, you look pretty today in your green dress.

SONG LEE: I like your green sparkly earrings.

MISS MACKLE: (*Whispers.*) Thank you, girls.

NARRATOR: Miss Mackle rocked in her chair as she turned to the right page.

SFX: *Krikkity krikk! Krikkity krekk!*

MISS MACKLE: 'Twas the night before Christmas
When all through the house
Not a creature was stirring
Not even a mmmm . . . "

NARRATOR: Suddenly, the bottom fell out of the rocking chair.

MISS MACKLE: *WHOOOOOOOOOOPS!* (*Falls off chair.*)

PROPS MANAGER: (*Drops three wooden blocks at the same time into an empty metal wastebasket.*)

HARRY: (*Stands up.*) Mayday! Mayday! Teacher on the floor!

SONG LEE: (*Stands up and puts her hand over her heart.*) Oh, no! Miss Mackle fell down!

MISS MACKLE: I sure did! What a whoopsy doodle!

HARRY: Good thing you didn't land on your noodle.

DOUG: (*Aside.*) I covered my eyes. I didn't want to picture the teacher standing on her head.

NARRATOR: Harry was the first one out of his seat to help the teacher.

HARRY: (*Runs in place.*)

DOUG: The rest of us gathered around. All of us dropped our jaws and gasped.

ALL: (*Everyone stands up, drops jaws, then gasps.*) Aaaaugh!

HARRY: Are you okay, Miss Mackle?

MISS MACKLE: Yes. I'm very thankful I managed to fall gracefully. I could be standing on my head. (*Looks at Harry.*) Or my noodle. (*Smiles.*) Thanks for helping me up.

HARRY: (*Makes a toothy smile.*) Come on, guys! Let's put these broken chair parts into the wastepaper basket. Mr. Beausoleil will figure out what to do with them.

SONG LEE: I'll help.

MARY/IDA/SID/DOUG: Me, too.

PROPS MANAGER: (*Drops wooden blocks into metal wastepaper basket one at a time.*)

ALL: (*Everyone sits back down.*)

MISS MACKLE: Now we just need to round up our globe. I knocked it over when I fell. And my green earring.

SONG LEE: I see your green sparkly earring, Miss Mackle.

MISS MACKLE: Where?

SONG LEE: In the fish tank.

HARRY: I'll get it. (*Rolls up his sleeve.*)

SIDNEY: Euewee . . . gross!

SFX: *Blub! Blub! Blub!*

HARRY: Here it is, good as new, Miss Mackle.

MARY: You mean good and smelly — and fishy.

SIDNEY: (*Holds nose.*) P. U.

NARRATOR: Just then, the principal showed up at the door holding a globe.

MR. CARDINI: (*Stands up.*) Anybody missing the world?

ALL: We are!

MR. CARDINI: Okay, then, it's yours. I found it rolling down the hallway.

MARY: Mr. Cardini, Miss Mackle fell on the floor! Her old rocking chair broke!

MR. CARDINI: Are you okay, Miss Mackle?

MISS MACKLE: Just fine, thanks to all my good helpers.

ALL: (*Everyone smiles.*)

IDA: Are you going to finish the story, Miss Mackle?

MR. CARDINI: What story are you reading?

ALL: "A Visit from St. Nicholas."

MARY: By Clement C. Moore.

IDA: It's almost two hundred years old.

MR. CARDINI: Wow! Well, I haven't heard it yet this year. May I join you?

ALL: YEESS!

SONG LEE: Here's a chair for you.

MR. CARDINI: Thank you, Song Lee. (*Sits down*.)

MISS MACKLE: Good! Now, since all of you are such wonderful helpers, why don't you help me read this holiday classic?

ALL: (*Clap and cheer*.)

NARRATOR: Miss Mackle began reading.

MISS MACKLE: 'Twas the night before . . .

ALL: *Christmas*

MISS MACKLE: When all through the . . .

ALL: *House*

MISS MACKLE: Not a creature was . . .

ALL: *Stirring*

MISS MACKLE: Not even a . . .

ALL: *Mouse.*

MR. CARDINI: (*Squeaks like a mouse.*)

HARRY: (*Squeaks like a mouse.*)

IDA/MARY/SONG LEE: (*Giggle.*)

SIDNEY: (*Laughs and snorts.*)

DOUG: (*Aside*) Room 2B is full of sounds. A few of them may be horrible, but most of them are fun.

ALL: HAPPY HOLIDAYS!

HARRY: Ho! Ho! Ho!

Want to finish reading "A Visit from St. Nicholas"? Just turn the page!

A Visit from St. Nicholas

By Clement Clarke Moore

'Twas the night before Christmas,
 when all through the house
Not a creature was stirring,
 not even a mouse.
The stockings were hung by the
 chimney with care,
In hopes that St. Nicholas soon
 would be there.

The children were nestled all snug
 in their beds,

While visions of sugar-plums danced
    in their heads.
And Mama in her 'kerchief, and I in my cap,
had just settled our brains
    for a long winter's nap;

When out on the lawn there arose
    such a clatter,
I sprang from my bed
    to see what was the matter.
Away to the window I flew like a flash,
Tore open the shutters
    and threw up the sash.

The moon on the breast of the
    new-fallen snow
Gave the lustre of mid-day to objects below,
when, what to my wondering eyes
    should appear,
but a miniature sleigh, and eight tiny
    reindeer.

With a little old driver, so lively
    and quick,
I knew in a moment it must be
    St. Nick.
More rapid than eagles his coursers
    they came,

And he whistled, and shouted, and called
   them by name:

"Now, Dasher! Now, Dancer! Now, Prancer
   and Vixen!
On, Comet! On, Cupid! On, Donder
   and Blitzen!
To the top of the porch! To the top of the
   wall!
Now dash away! Dash away! Dash away all!"

As dry leaves that before the wild
   hurricane fly,
when they meet with an obstacle, mount
   to the sky
so up to the house-top the coursers they flew,
with a sleigh full of toys, and St. Nicholas
   too.
And then, in a twinkling, I heard on the
   roof
The prancing and pawing of each little
   hoof.
As I drew in my head, and was turning
   around,
down the chimney St. Nicholas came with
   a bound.

He was dressed all in fur, from his head
    to his foot,
and his clothes were all tarnished with
    ashes and soot.
A bundle of toys he had flung on his back,
And he looked like a peddler just opening
    his pack.

His eyes — how they twinkled! His dimples,
    how merry!
His cheeks were like roses, his nose like
    a cherry!
His droll little mouth was drawn up like
    a bow,
and the beard of his chin was as white
    as the snow;

The stump of a pipe he held tight in his
    teeth,
and the smoke it encircled his head
    like a wreath;
He had a broad face and a little round belly,
    that shook when he laughed, like
    a bowl full of jelly.

He was chubby and plump, a right jolly
    old elf,
And I laughed when I saw him,

in spite of myself.
A wink of his eye and a twist of his head,
Soon gave me to know I had nothing
   to dread.

He spoke not a word, but went straight
   to his work,
And fill'd all the stockings, then turned
   with a jerk,
And laying his finger aside of his nose,
And giving a nod, up the chimney he rose.

He sprang to his sleigh, to his team gave a
   whistle,
And away they all flew like the down of a
   thistle.
But I heard him exclaim, ere he drove
   out of sight,
"Happy Christmas to all and to all
   a good night."

About the Authors

Stephanie Calmenson ("Take a Penny, Leave a Penny") is the author of more than one hundred books. She lives in New York City with her dog, Rosie, a Tibetan terrier whose training to become a working dog she wrote about in *Rosie: A Visiting Dog's Story*.

Debbie Dadey and **Marcia Thornton Jones** ("Holiday Disaster") are the authors of the bestselling series The Adventures of the Bailey School Kids and Ghostville Elementary. They met when they taught together at the same elementary school. They now live in different states, but write together using the "hot potato" method of writing, trading a story back and forth until it's ready to become a book.

Suzy Kline ("The Rocking Chair") taught elementary school for almost thirty years. Now she has retired from teaching and writes full-time. She is the author of the Horrible Harry and Song Lee series, which are available from Penguin Putnam. She has two grown-up daughters. Suzy lives in Connecticut.

Clement Clarke Moore ("A Visit from St. Nicholas") was born in New York City in 1779. He graduated from Columbia University in 1798 and went on to become a professor at the General Theological Seminary of the Protestant Episcopal Church. He wrote "A Visit from St. Nicholas" in 1822, but his identity as the author remained a secret until 1844. He died in Newport, Rhode Island, in 1863, just before his eighty-fourth birthday.

James Preller ("The Case of the Santa Claus Mystery") is the author of the popular Jigsaw Jones mystery series and many other books. He lives in Delmar, New York, with his wife, Lisa, three children (Nick, Gavin, and Maggie), one dog, one cat, and a tankful of fancy-tailed guppies.

Barbara Seuling ("Wally's First Christmas") is an author and illustrator of fiction, nonfiction, and picture books. She is perhaps best known for her Robert books, which began with *Oh No, It's Robert*. She was born in Brooklyn, New York, and currently splits her time between New York City and Vermont.

Sue Wright ("The Nutcracker Retold," "Midnight Gets a Star," "Christmas on the Prairie") lives in Liberty, Missouri, with her husband, Dick, and their cats, Mother and Baby. They have five grown children and ten grandchildren. She worked for many years as a social worker, specializing in adoptions and working with foster children. She published her first book with Scholastic, *The Christmas Path*, in 1998.